ALSO BY WALTER ABISH:

Duel Site, Tibor de Nagy Editions, 1970
Alphabetical Africa, New Directions, 1974
Minds Meet, New Directions, 1975
In the Future Perfect, New Directions, 1977
How German Is It, New Directions, 1980

Walter Abish

99: THE NEW MEANING

with photographs by Cecile Abish

BURNING DECK
Providence

The texts in this book first appeared in Conjunctions,
Personal Injury *and* Renegade.

*This project is in part supported by a grant from the
Rhode Island State Council on the Arts.*

**Library of Congress
Cataloging-in-Publication Data**

Abish, Walter
   99: the new meaning / Walter Abish.
     p. cm.
   Contents: What else — Inside out — Skin deep —
Reading Kafka in German — 99: the new meaning.
   ISBN 0-930901-67-3: $20.00.
   ISBN 0-930901-66-5 (pbk.): $8.00.
   ISBN 0-930901-68-1 (signed): $30.00
   I. Title. II. Title: 99: the new meaning.
PS3551.B5N5   1990
813'.54—dc20   89-22349
                                       CIP

CONTENTS

These works were undertaken in a playful spirit—not actually "written" but orchestrated. The fragmented narrative can be said to function as a kind of lure—given the constraints, anything else would be beyond its scope. In using selected segments of published texts authored by others as the exclusive "ready made" material for these five "explorations," I wanted to probe certain familiar emotional configurations afresh, and arrive at an emotional content that is not mine by design. The titlepiece, "99: The New Meaning," consisting of no less than 99 segments by as many authors, each line, sentence or paragraph appropriated from a page bearing that same, to me, mystically significant number 99, and the European pseudo-autobiography, "What Else," obtained from 50 self-portraits, journals, diaries, and collected letters, ineluctably led to the subsequent fictional probes on Flaubert and Kafka.

The numbers above each segment of the five literary probes indicate the total of "appropriated" words from each independent source.

"Skin Deep" was largely inspired by the sexual bravado of Flaubert's letters and travel notes, the pleasurably eroticized depiction of Flaubert's Tunisian stay providing the right note for this literary infringement, while "Reading Kafka in German" was an attempt to have Kafka's disturbing and often uncanny prescience activate and determine the reading of the 99 appropriated segments. In giving shape to the Kafka piece I was stimulated by the emblematic K. of *The Castle*, a "K." singular in that the use of the initial

voided any necessity to provide or explain the character's
antecedents. Kafka's marked disinclination to furnish K.'s
credentials—K. has no identifiable or censoriously traceable
past—greatly contributed to the heightened immediacy of
The Castle.

All selections from books by foreign authors were made
from their American translations—most of the segments for
"Skin Deep" and "Reading Kafka in German" were culled
from works by French and German language authors
respectively.

I have omitted the names of the 18th, 19th and 20th century sources from which the segments were obtained, not
wishing to add to or distract from the newly synthesized
texts. In each case, the challenge was to generate a self-
contained work that advanced a picture, especially one not
inimical to the one I have of these two major literary figures, Flaubert and Kafka.

Walter Abish
New York, February 6, 1989

WHAT
ELSE

PART I

95

I was twenty. I will let no one say it is the best time of life.
Everything threatens a young man with ruin: love, ideas,
the loss of his family, his entrance into the world of adults.
It is hard to learn one's part in the world.

What was our world like? It was the chaos the Greeks
put at the beginning of the universe in the midst of creation.
Except that we thought it was the beginning of the end, the
real end, and not the one that is the beginning of a beginning.

100

Often memories are nothing. As though a window curtain
were to remain intact during a fire, the silliest images come
down from the attic of recollections, while momentous ones
remain there. One of my great memories is of having

filched out of my grandfather's bedroom, after he died, a
package of dreadful cigarettes, Nazilles or Nazirs, I can't
remember which, and some kind of cigarette holder. I pock-
eted them all, and can still see myself at Maisons-Lafitte,
among the paths and tall grass of the Place Sully, smoking
that cigarette with the sovereign awareness of disobeying. I
was happy.

92
I was told I was good looking and believed it. For some time
I had a white speck in my right eye which was to blind it
and make me squint; but this was not yet apparent. Hun-
dreds of photographs were taken of me and my mother
touched them up with colored pencils. In one, which has sur-
vived, I am fair and pink, with curls, my cheeks are plump
and I am wearing a look of kindly deference to the established order; my mouth is swollen with hypocrisy: I know
my worth.

79
I keep beginning again. I keep taking a fresh notebook.
And each time I hope it will lead to something, that it will be
a constructive experiment, that I shall open some door. It
never happens. I stop before I get to a door, any door. The
same invisible obstacle that stops me. I ought at least to try
and keep the same notebook, to get to the last page. That
would mean that I have said almost everything.

157
Yet I exist. Not of course, as an individual, since in this
respect I am merely the stake—a stake perpetually at
risk—in the struggle between another society, made up of
several thousand million nerve cells lodged in the ant hill of
my skull, and my body, which serves as its robot. Neither
psychology nor metaphysics nor art can provide me with a
refuge. There are myths, now open to internal investigation

by a new kind of sociology which will emerge one day and
will deal more gently with them than traditional sociology
does. The self is not only hateful: there is no place between
us and *nothing*. And if, in the last resort, I opt for *us*, even
though it is no more than a semblance, the reason is that,
unless I destroy myself—an act which would obliterate the
conditions of the option—I have only one possible choice between this semblance and nothing.

132

I had taken an apartment at the back of a house, all the
windows overlooking the court. On purpose! For one thing, I
can't stand light, can't stand being drenched in strong natu-
ral rays; but then, too, in order to hide from men and
women. "Always polite" was my slogan, "but few appear-
ances and never without preparation." I had no telephone
either, to make appointments impossible. I went to the usu-
al parties, clinked glasses with the men, ran through the
standard gossip with the ladies, and never let the flower girl
pass without buying the bunch in season for the lady on
your right. I don't think anyone thought of considering me
improper. Of course, there was a lot of calculation and su-
perstructures in all this, yet that was my own business.

169

My chief activity, literature, a term disparged today. I do
not hesitate to use it, however, for it is a question of fact:
one is a literary man as one is a botanist, a philosopher, an
astronomer, a physicist, a doctor. There is no point in in-
venting other terms, other excuses to justify one's predilec-
tion for writing: anyone who likes to think with a pen is a
writer. The few books I have published, however, won me
no fame. I do not complain of this, anymore than I brag of
it, for I feel the same distaste for the "popular author" genre
as for that of the "neglected poet."
Without being a traveler in the strict sense of the word, I

have seen a certain number of cities: as a young man,
Switzerland, Belgium, Holland, England; later, the Rhine-
land, Egypt, Greece, Italy and Spain; quite recently equato-
rial Africa. Yet I speak no foreign language fluently and
this fact, along with others, gives me a sense of inadequacy
and isolation.

198
I have long, indeed for years, played with the idea of setting
out the sphere of life—bios—graphically on a map. First I
envisaged an ordinary map, but now I would incline to a
general staff's map of a city center, if such a thing existed.
Doubtless, it does not, because of the ignorance of the thea-
tre of future wars. I have evolved a system of signs, and on
the gray background of such maps they would make a color-
ful show if I clearly marked in the houses of my friends and
girlfriends, the assembly halls of various collectives, from
the "debating chambers" of the Youth Movement to the
gathering places of the Communist youth, the hotel and
brothel rooms that I knew for one night, the decisive
beaches in the Tiergarten, the ways to the different schools
and the graves I saw filled, the sites of the prestigious cafés
whose long forgotten names daily crossed our lips, the tennis
courts where empty apartment blocks stand today, and the
halls emblazoned with gold and stucco that the terrors of
dancing classes made almost the equal of gymnasiums.

69
3 January. Epigraphs for the whole of my diaries:
a) Pascal, 71 & 72, in the Chevalier's editing. Montaigne's
". . . je suis moy-mesmes la matiere de mon livre. . ."
b) the opening of Kenko's Tsurezure-gusa: What a strange
demented feeling it gives me when I realize that I have
spent whole days before this inkstone, with nothing better to
do, jotting down at random whatever nonsensical thoughts
have entered my head!

274
Sunrise is a necessary concomitant of long railway journeys, just as are hard boiled eggs, illustrated papers, packs of cards, rivers upon which boats strain but make no progress. At a certain moment when I was turning over the thoughts that had filled my mind, in the preceding minutes, so as to discover whether I had just been asleep or not (and when the very uncertainty which made me ask myself the question was to furnish me with an affirmative answer), in the pale square of the window, over a small black wood I saw some ragged clouds whose fleecy edges were a fixed dead-pink not liable to change, like the color that dyes the wing which has grown to wear it, or the sketch upon which the artist's fancy has washed it. But I felt that, unlike them, this color was due neither to inertia nor to caprice but to necessity and life. Presently there gathered behind it reserves of light. It brightened; the sky turned to crimson which I strove, gluing my eyes to the window, to see more clearly, for I felt that it was related somehow to the most intimate life of nature, but, the course of the line altering, the train turned, the morning scene gave place in the frame of the window to a nocturnal village, its roofs still blue with moonlight, its ponds encrusted with the opalescent nacre of night, beneath a firmament still powdered with all its stars, and I was lamenting the loss of my strip of pink sky when I caught sight of it afresh, but red this time in the opposite window.

97
From the past, it is my childhood which fascinates me most; these images alone, upon inspection, fail to make me regret the time which has vanished. For it is not the irreversible I discover in childhood, it is the irreducible: everything which is still in me, by fits and starts; in the child I read quite openly the dark underside of myself — boredom, vulnera-

bility, disposition to despair (in the plural, fortunately), inward excitement, cut off (unfortunately) from all expression.

Contemporaries: I was beginning to walk, Proust was still alive, and finishing *A la Recherche du Temps Perdu.*

92

It is not for me to ponder what is happening to the "shape of a city," even if the true city distracted and abstracted from the one I live in by the force of an element which is to my mind what air is supposed to be to life. Without regret, at this moment I see it change and even disappear. It slides, it burns, it sinks into the shudder of weeds along its barricades, into the dreams of curtains in its bedroom, where a man and a woman indifferently continue making love.

36

March 11

How time flies; another ten days and I have achieved nothing. It doesn't come off. A page now and then is successful, but I can't keep it up, the next day I am powerless.

49

My principle objection wasn't the *vanity* involved in writing one's autobiography. Such books are like others: quickly forgotten if boring. What I was frightened of was deflowering the happy moments I've experienced by describing and dissecting them. Now that's what I certainly will *not* do—I'll skip them instead.

132

It must have been fine outside. The windows with their heavy curtains greasy with dust, gave unto a cool, shaded courtyard, as echoing as a well. At the end of this courtyard a man was clearing his throat; he cleared it carefully, for a long time, spat, and then began to sing quietly. The

afternoon had that particular resonance which a very blue
sky seems to give to Paris when it is rather empty. I was
lying there, stretched out in silence, with my body calm and
relaxed and the pleasant smell of a cigarette in my mouth,
and I saw that afternoon (just as I had for the first time
seen a painting); saw it purposeless, not devoid of charm,
but unrelated to anything, floating like a flower on the
water.

122
As far back as I remember myself (with interest, with
amusement, seldom with admiration or disgust), I have been
subject to mild hallucinations. Some are aural, others are
optical and by none have I profited much. The fatidic ac-
cents that restrained Socrates or egged on Joaneta Darc
have degenerated with me to the level of something one happens to hear between lifting and clapping down the receiver
of a busy party-line telephone. Just before falling asleep, I
often become aware of a kind of one-sided conversation going
on in an adjacent section of my mind, quite independently
from the actual trend of my thoughts. It is a neutral,
detached, anonymous voice, which I catch saying words of
no importance whatever.

73
My only desire, at one time, was to be in the police. It
seemed to me a fitting occupation for my sleepless, intri-
guing mind. I imagined that among criminals there were
people worth fighting with, clever, crafty, desperate people.
Later I recognized that it was a good thing that I gave up
the idea; for almost everything the police have to deal with
is concerned with poverty and misery—not criminals or
gangsters.

113

When I was ten I went to the opera for the first time. They were playing *Il Trovatore*, and I was struck by the fact that these people suffered so much and that they were never calm and seldom gay. But I quickly felt at home in the pathetic style. I began to like the ravings of Leonora, and when her hands fumbled wildly about her mouth, I felt I recognized in this gesture a desperate grab at her dentures; I even saw the glitter of a few outflung teeth. In the Bible people used to rent their garments; why shouldn't pulling out your teeth be a beautiful and moving expression of despair?

168

All the abandoned cities and towns and beach resorts that keep returning to my fiction were there in that huge landscape, the area just around our camp, which was about seven or eight miles from Shanghai, out in the paddy fields in a former university. There was a period when we didn't know the war had ended, when the Japanese had more or less abandoned the whole zone and the Americans had yet to come in, then all of the images I keep using—the abandoned apartment houses and so forth—must have touched something in my mind. It was a very interesting zone psychologically, and it obviously has a big influence—as did the semi-tropical nature of the place: lush vegetation, a totally water-logged world, huge rivers, canals, paddies, great sheets of water everywhere. It was a dramatized landscape thanks to the war and to the collapse of the irrigation system—a landscape dramatized in a way that is difficult to find in say, Western Europe.

168

Her apartment: for reasons that are no longer clear to me, a few weeks after that first evening in her apartment, we moved the convertible couch from the north wall of the living room to the west wall. After we parted, but before we were married, the furniture was moved once again, as if to erase my former presence. I can understand the movement of the furniture as well as and as passionately as I understand Schubert's sonatas. The aquarium with its dozen guppies was by now long gone. After we were married but living apart, she once again moved the couch. I often wonder if I avoided sleeping with her after we were married for the sake of the text-to-be? I believe she had not read *The Sun Also Rises* but her parting words seemed straight out of that all too familiar exchange in the novel. Am I reading into her parting gift, Malraux's *The Voices of Silence*, a meaning that wasn't there? Why write?

135
I have not kept a journal for more than a year. I have lost the habit. I did not exactly promise myself to resume it, but all the same, I should like to try; for in the state in which I am at present, I fear that any other attempted production will be destined to failure. I have just reread with disgust a few pages I had written at Neuchatel; they smack of effort, and the tone strikes me as stilted. Doubtless they were not written naturally and they betray an anxiety to escape certain reproaches, which it is absurd to take into account. My great strength, even in the past, was being very little concerned with opinion and not trying to construct myself consistently; writing as simply as possible and without trying to prove anything.

97
I went down to have a look at the lake, and to see if it was doing anything wild. It wasn't. I went out of a sense of duty towards it. I have lost all pleasure in the lake, and indeed in the woods, since the soldiers came and invaded them and robbed them of all the privacy I so loved. You didn't understand when I minded the tanks cutting up the

wild flowers. It was a thing of beauty now tarnished for ever—one of the few things I had preserved against the horrible new world.

111

I have a shelf on top of one of my bookcases at home that has my books—the first hardbound copy of each of my books that I have received (I believe ten of them in all). Each of them is significant to me; they have become totemic. I wrote my name in them and put them away. I have these ten books all in one place. And every once in a while, I look at them, especially the first ten, with a real sense of pleasure. I want to touch them. Sometimes I smell them. I like the smell—they are no longer fresh, some of them being very old.

115

Cora was lost, my marriage had failed, nothing had come of an attempted reconciliation. A mountain of rustling crackling paper remained behind in the room. Nothing had been made to last by these papers. I stood in a square in the center of the city, in a sharply outlined space lit by the sun in the middle of a crater of shadows, the pages of a torn newspaper fluttering across the main street in the gusty wind.

Irresolutely I went to the travel agency, stood for a while in front of the window, then walked in and only when the assistant behind the counter turned to me, did Paris occur to me as a destination.

41
July 31
One can imagine a face for the void. Then it strikes us how much the void resembles us. Is it myself I am staring at?
The dark is checked by the dark, as a hand by a stranger's hand.

70

As night fell, we were standing in the garden; deep in
thought, we were almost motionless, at the most shifting our
weight from one foot to the other, now and then. From time
to time, one of us took a sip of wine from a glass that
seemed forgotten the moment he picked it up. We were so
drained of emotion that sometimes we were afraid of drop-
ping our glasses.

88

Here is a whole nervous breakdown in miniature. We came
on Tuesday. Sank into a chair, could scarcely rise; everything insipid; tasteless, colorless. Enormous desire for rest.
Wednesday—only wish to be alone in the open air. Air deli-
cious—avoided speech; could not be read. Thought of my
own power of writing with veneration, as of something in-
credible, belonging to someone else never again to be
annoyed by one. Mind a blank. Slept in my chair. Thurs-
day. No pleasure in life whatsoever; but felt perhaps more
attuned to existence.

49

Dec. 20. Nothing so stupid as a journal, when you go scrib-
bling in it without any real want. There is no pleasure in
keeping a diary when you cannot lock it in a drawer and
when absolutely anyone can read it every morning without
undertanding a word of it.

74

Even when we got happily swished and threw dishes out of
the kitchen window—only to find them unbroken when the
snows cleared—I was shocked by the satisfied violence with
which she proclaimed an end to our marriage. I was a
"three-time loser," which was obviously true. I heard it
with relief. There was no doubt about it. I was not good at
this marriage business. I looked forward to lonely freedom.

74

18 July

My dear Walter

As you see, I am still writing from here, and nothing came of the Scandinavian journey! I couldn't help smiling because I seem to notice that you are turning my own weapon against me. Heaven knows what you hit, but certainly not the "enemy"! What is all this about the soul? Or a Scandinavian journey? The most that could have done for me is provide me with some distraction.

PART II

198

I was on an English boat going from Siracusa in Sicily to Tunis in North Africa. I had taken the cheapest passage and it was a voyage of two nights and one day. We were no sooner out of the harbor that I found that in my class no food was served. I sent a note to the captain saying I'd like to change to another class. He sent a note back saying that I could not change and, further, asking whether I had been vaccinated. I wrote back that I had not been vaccinated and that I didn't intend to be. He wrote back that unless I was vaccinated I would not be permitted to disembark at Tunis. We had meanwhile gotten in a terrific storm. The waves were higher than the boat. It was impossible to walk on the deck. The correspondence between the captain and myself continued in a deadlock. In my last note to him, I stated my firm intention to get off his boat at the earliest opportunity and without being vaccinated. He then wrote back that I had been vaccinated and to prove it he sent along a certificate with his signature.

66

The writer of this book is no misanthrope; today one pays too dearly for hatred of man. If one would hate man the way man was hated formerly, Timonically, wholly, without exception, with a full heart, and with the whole love of hatred, then one would have to renounce contempt. And how much fine joy, how much graciousness ever do we owe precisely to our contempt!

121

I play my role. Only in the plane or hotel into which promoters have booked me am I for a while alone and under no obligation to maintain anything. I take a bath or a shower, then stand at the window—a view of another city. A twinge of stage fright, every time. While reading, I forget each word the moment I have read it. Afterward a cold buffet. To the same questions I do not always return the same answers, for I do not find any of my answers all that convincing. I watch a lady's nice teeth from close up as she speaks to me; I hold a glass in my hand, and I sweat. This is not my metier, I think to myself, but here I stand.

85

Sometimes the weary traveler suffering from jetlag prefers to be shown directly to his hotel to be sewn in the sheets from which no dreams ever befalls. Weary and heartsick, emotionally battered by the voyage, the eyes overcome with fatigue, unable to read the newspaper thoughtfully provided for him he teeters on the hem of sleep, disrobing this way or that, clenching in his teeth all these distraught objects of the recent past—the way someone looked at him, seeming not seeing but just seeing.

83
Since I have been famous, neckties, caps, handkerchiefs, and whole sentences complete with instruction for use have been stolen from me. (Fame is someone it seems to be fun to piss on.) The more famous a man gets the fewer friends he has. It can't be helped: fame isolates. When fame helps you he never lets you forget it. When he hurts you, he says something about the price you have to pay. I certify that fame is boring and only rarely amusing.

195
Sousse, Sfax, the great Ranan circus at El Djem, Kairouan, Djerba—I reach them all without difficulty by train, by bus and by boat. At Djerba, Ulysses had forgotten Penelope and Ithaca: the island was worthy of its legend. It was a cool orchard with a carpet of dappled grass; the glossy crowns of palms sheltered by the delicate blossoming trees; the edges of this garden were lashed by the sea. I was the only guest at the hotel and the owner spoiled me. She told me that the summer before, one of her boarders, a little English girl, had gone every day to a deserted beach to lie in the sun; one day she came back to lunch, her face all crumpled, and did not touch her food. "What's the matter?" my hostess asked; the girl burst into tears. Three Arabs who had been watching her for several days, had raped her, one by one. "I tried to cheer her up," the woman said. "I said to her: Oh! Mademoiselle, when you are travelling. . . Come now, calm yourself; after all, when you are travelling!" But she insisted on packing her bags that same evening.

92
A disturbed night in spite of the pill. Dreamt angrily of someone of whom I have never waking thought angrily.
    Conrad's *Heart of Darkness* still a fine story, but its faults show now. The language too inflated for the situation. Kurtz never really comes alive. It is as if Conrad had taken

an episode in his own life and tried to lend it, for the sake of "literature," a greater significance than it will hold. And how often he compares something concrete with something abstract. Is this a trick I have caught.

45
June 22.
Now the itch to write is over, the vacuum in my brain begins again. My novel is finished, I feel a twinge of rheumatism or arthritis. Is it that you can feel only one thing at a time, or do you imagine them?

154
The day before yesterday we were in the house of a woman who had two others there for us to lay. The place was delapidated and open to all the winds and lit by the night-light, we could see a palm tree through the unglassed window, and two Turkish women wore silk robes embroidered with gold. This is a great place for contrasts: splendid things gleaming in the dust. I performed on a mat that a family of cats had to be shooed off—a strange coitus, looking at each other without being able to exchange a word, and the exchange of looks is all the deeper for the curiosity and surprise. My brain was too stimulated for me to enjoy it otherwise. These shaved cunts make a strange effect—the flesh is as hard as bronze, and my girl has a splendid arse.

Goodbye—Write to me, write to my mother sometimes...

148
Oct. 14
I get up early and go to the dining room for coffee. Everybody bows and I bow and I can't remember any of their names or what they are doing here. I know some of them are journalists, some of them are working for the government, and most of them are foreigners, but they swim as one except for a tall, pale young Frenchman and a German

couple who shake hands with affection as they part each morning in front of the hotel. I have done nothing since I am here and I recognize the signs. I have presented my credentials, as one must, gone once to the Press Office where I was pleasantly welcomed by Constancia de la Mora, had two telephone calls from her suggesting I come back to the office and meet people who might like to meet me, and have not gone.

143
Jackdaws inhabit the village. Two horses are feeding on the bark of a tree. Apples lie rotting in the wet clay soil around the trees, nobody is harvesting them. On one of the trees, which seemed from afar like the only tree left with any leaves, apples hung in mysterious clusters close to one another. There isn't a single leaf on the wet tree, just wet apples refusing to fall. I picked one, it tasted pretty sour, but the juice in it quenched my thirst. I threw the apple core against the tree, and the apples fell like rain. When the apples had becalmed again, restful on the ground, I thought to myself that no one could imagine such human loneliness. It is the loneliest day, the most isolated of all. So I went and shook the tree until it was utterly bare.

111
Back from Morocco, I once sat down with eyes closed and legs crossed in a corner of my room and tried to say "Allah! Allah! Allah!" over and over again for half-an-hour at the right speed and volume. I tried to imagine myself going on saying it for a whole day and a large part of the night; taking a short sleep and then beginning again; doing the same thing for days and weeks, months and years; growing older and older and living like that, and clinging tenaciously to that life; flying into a fury if something disturbed me in that life; wanting nothing else, sticking to it utterly.

97

There is something else too. When Doughty went to Arabia
in the 1800s, he claimed somewhat grandly that it was to
revive the expressive possibilities of the English language.
Well, in a sense, I also went to the desert to solve a problem
with language, although not as Doughty meant it. Perhaps I
can put it this way. It's possible to think of language as the
most versatile, and maybe the original, form of deception, a
sort of fortunate fall: I lie and am lied to, but the result of
my lie is mental leaps, memory, knowledge.

196

We got up and wandered across the square, looking at some
acrobats and musicians, but as soon as one of the perform-
ers spotted us as tourists, he would rush over to demand
money before we had even seen anything. We tried to
watch a snake charmer who was holding a snake by the
neck a few inches from his mouth, almost licking it with his
tongue, while an assistant was beating a drum. He spotted
us and right away came over for money. We gave him a 50
francs piece which he looked at with disdain. He brought
over a snake and asked us to touch it. It felt stangely cool
and smooth in spite of the slight roughness of its tiny scales.
It would bring us good luck, he said. We gave him a 100
franc piece, whereupon with an unpleasant grin he hung the
snake around poor Edwin's neck, stroking its head, saying
that it would make him rich and always keep him out of
trouble with the police. I gave him another 100 francs so he
would take the snake off Edwin's neck and before he could
put it around mine, we fled.

78

Friday 12th

Eating cherries today in front of the mirror I saw my idiotic
face. Those self-contained bullets disappearing down my
mouth made it look looser, more lascivious and contradictory

than ever. It contains many elements of brutality, calm, slackness, boldness and cowardice, but as elements only, and it is more changeable and characterless than a landscape beneath scurrying clouds. That's why so many people find it so impossible to retain (You've too many of them, says Hedda).

137
6 Oct
Since I arrived in Paris, there isn't a day that goes by that I don't window-shop in the bookstores. Sometimes I even go in to look through the shelves of books on display. And bit by bit I am feeling a profound distaste for literature. I don't really know what its origin is. Is it the enormous number of books that are appearing, the thousands of novels translated from every language, and somewhat at random (for Eca de Queiroz, Pio Baroja, Rebreanu, etc., are still unknown)? Complete anarchy, chaos. And the artificial production of the "new wave." This too: a novel no longer interests the modern critic unless it's difficult, almost unreadable; or unless it illustrates a new thoery of the novel or literature.

100
The cliché that clichés are cliché only because their truth is self-evident would seem self-evident. Yet from birth we're taught that things are not simple as they seem. The wise man's work is to undo complications: things are simple, truth blazes ("brightness falls from the air"), and the obvious way to prevent wars is not to fight. Thus, when I proclaim that I am never less alone than when I am by myself, and am met with a glazed stare, the stare is from one who abhors a vacuum—the look of nature. But I am complicating matters.

106
Yesterday I tried to let myself go completely. The result was that I fell into a deep sleep and experienced nothing except a great sense of refreshment, and the curious sensation of having seen something important while I was asleep. But what it was I could not remember; it had gone forever.

But today this pencil will prevent my going to sleep. I dimly see certain strange images that seem to have no connection with my past; an engine puffing up a steep incline dragging endless coaches after it. Where can it all come from? Where is it going? How did it get there at all?

13
Jean Jacques Rousseau confesses himself. It is less a need than an idea.

46
What tense would you choose to live in?
I want to live in the imperative of the future passive participle—in the "what ought to be."

I like to breathe that way. That's what I like. It suggests a kind of mounted, bandit-like equestrian honor. . .

INSIDE
OUT

30
At six in the afternoon the first automobile appeared on the road, the fright of the birds was translated into an agitated beating of wings directed toward the nearby forest.

41
The Fort lay in the center of the district we had to survey. Our northern territory occupied a large part of it, between the Teshangani and the Givelor rivers, whither it was our duty to go during two months in the year.

16
I must say until astonishment came, I got nothing but pleasure out of the little expedition.

21
Perhaps life needs to be deciphered like a cryptogram, secret staircases, frames from which the paintings quickly slip aside and vanish. . .

44
Madeline (off): What is the center of the world for you?
Paul: The center of the world?
Madeline (off): Yes.
Paul: It's funny. I mean we've never spoken to each other
and the first time we talk, you ask me such a surprising
question.

41
Afterwards a light rain of ashes falls. Small viscous clots
float in the air. Spider web fragments with a faintly nauseating odor like bromine. That is all that remains of man.
There is nothing to do but love each other passionately.

32
The communication comes from the south in lead pencil.
"There will be a system of communications. We are to
induct those who collide in the exits without falling. Evalu-
ate this, Alu Baris."

32
The deplorable sequel has shown only too well how right he
had been to mistrust us, how fully justified the following
Sunday was that hesitant pause before he broke into a
laugh.

18
At the crack of the gun he rose an inch or two, as if he had
been struck.

25
Would you like to know how Charlotte got those nine
stitches, I asked suddenly, in a tone of voice that sounded
perfectly normal to me.

22
He couldn't get rid of the key. I advised him simply to
throw the key away. I knew he wouldn't do it.

14
She pushed aside the roll tray he offered her, "you recognize
me, don't you?"

24
The eye keeps returning to the white Formica, because it
stands out. The perfect world of Formica, thinks George. It
is an agreeable surface.

8
What is thought, but disease of action.

20
Why didn't you say before that you were married.
It's an old story now, I thought there was no need.

6
Her breasts are again half exposed.

36
Do these lines perplex you? So did your letter. What kind of
an explanation is this—your "trip to the country!" Doubts
may be a good spur to the imagination, but you may have
abused it and me.

25
I'm no different as an author from all authors who ever
existed since man first began to write. Using other devises,
but analagous ones.

9
How do you mean all this, truthfully or ironically?

21
I am a timorous man. I can say it now that I have brought
my incredibly risky plan to an end.

21
You will understand that this is a postcard that someone
found in a drawer and decided to use as a joke.

12
From which I have learnt the full measure of the word
"vision."

23
Her face has regular, strongly marked features. Her hair is
black. But her eyes are pale, a color between blue-green and
pale-blue.

25
Why are you so tense, Hengel?
Are you being funny?
Look at your hand. It's so tight. And look at your skin.
Your skin's terrible.

14
You rang this bell by pressing your finger against it. That's
what you did.

8
The neighbors are walking in the garden. Smiling.

15
It is a crucial scene. How it was actually resolved I must
try and remember.

27
As for what actually happened, I don't quite remember
except that he gave me two or three claps, which it would be
impolite to mention to you.

3
She stood up.

7
Don't just stand there baby, do something.

43
Still René Leys said nothing. What tact. What a sense of
occasion. So it was for me to invade the silence and the
darkness. . . No, I continued my musing, and with even
greater clarity and lucidity than the midday sun upon the
rooftops.

15
But let me return to the world of the present and speak of
real events.

8
Oh yes, she said, I will, I will.

5
Yet impregnated as we are. . .

6
For you it is not enough.

17
She remembers the Astronaut John W. Young as he stepped
from the landing craft unto the moon.

7
I wondered a little. Honorable to whom?

8
Have you ever considered Melville's sex life?

21
My question produced in him a little gesture of elation, a
gesture emphasized by a snap of his forefinger and thumb.

5
I knew it was special.

30
We opened the eggs to let the yellow out. Bill was worried
about the white part, but we told him not to worry about
that. People do it every day.

4
Otherwise their intensity evaporated.

2
You're a. . . ?

48
These stairs, originally black, have rusted now to a beautiful
shade of green, due to some chemical element in the climate
in and surrounding Shanghai. These stairs are five hundred
yards tall. But we must hurry. For this city has innumerable stairways that are worthy of our attention.

11
We need to investigate and define the injury done to Gregor.

17
What a joke if at the end of this hunt he came face to face
with himself.

9
I don't think that will happen, I just don't.

7
The negative goal forces him to react.

11
The road we were to embark on had been abandoned.

39
Suppose I wanted to replace all the words of my language at
once by other ones; how could I tell the place where one of
the new words belong? Is it images that keep the places of
the word?

24
Branide: Do you think that some of the information contained in the messages will have meanings which are
beyond human experience?
Morrison: Surely, yes.

23
And then one day when he had been particularly insistent
she had given up and said: Oh, for Christ's sake go and see
for yourself.

37
A rather intricate key opened the sliding doors, the sides
folding back, to the kneeling observer appeared, on unpaint-
ed shelves, quiet and dustless, the expensive equipment one
can buy to fight the passage of time.

28

I entered Kafka's office. There was nobody there. Papers lying open. Two pears on a plate, a few newspapers were in evidence that he was in the building.

30

Ambivalence, that was something to have discovered—the sort of mingled revulsion and attraction, a coexistence in the same individual, with respect to the same object, of love and hatred.

30

The flecks of lung tissue speckled the bright ribbon of the rail. The bullet had broken two ribs, then collapsed her left lung and lodged itself below her scapula.

8

I'm afraid you've made a mistake, she answered.

8

He looked about him and counted the dead.

18

If you compare the previous frame with this frame, you will see how my wrist has snapped forward.

9

I want to wage war against everything that moves.

14

Don't kill me, please don't kill me! Don't kill me, please don't kill me.

12

During the long period we have been considering, three significant changes emerge:

27
I loathe unexpectedly catching sight of myself in a mirror, for unless I have prepared myself for the confrontation I seem humiliatingly ugly to myself each time.

10
The bedroom begins to shift from one identity to another.

4
The author is undecided.

25
This exiguous plot—if it can be called a plot at all—brings to the stage that tendency toward a narrative of purely horizontal line.

13
(I am breaking the process into its components for the sake of analysis)

15
You are located where this second line cuts the first.
You hurt me, she said.

15
I forgot to tell you that he had to leave by the small garden gate.

25
I was in the middle, hugging the envelope. I don't know how much of the garden we had crossed when we heard voices behind us.

39
Each of the two circular concrete towers had seven storeys, mostly under water, the lower levels of both towers

containing stores—fuel in one, fresh water in the other. The next level contained food, other general stores and munitions.

9
There was a tiny red flame on the sky.

41
The United States was paralyzed. No one knew what was happening. There were no newspapers, no letters, no dispatches. Every community was completely isolated as if ten thousand miles of primeval wilderness stretched between it and the rest of the world.

5
He lies sourly in bed.

32
Neither is there any end: you never leave a woman, a friend, a city in one go. And then everything looks alike: Shanghai, Moscow, Algiers, everything is the same after two weeks.

38
There was still no blood where the knife had sunk.
I am in a room alone with a dead man, she said to herself, as if it had nothing to do with her. Her breathing came in gasps.

26
It is altogether strange, but more and more I *feel* myself to be Mesopotamian. It is a terribly isolated feeling. I have no people as yet.

40

With the disappearance of my notebook I turned to the only
writing material at hand, some large sheets of paper I found
in the desk drawer and which I shall continue to use until
this whole matter is cleared up.

31

The more a story is told in a proper well-spoken straightfor-
ward way, in an even tone, the easier it is to reverse it, to
blacken it, to read it inside out.

SKIN
DEEP

43
The need to become familiar with Albertine's desire is so intense that the activity of loving turns out to be something like a compulsory intellectual investigation. And the detective-story atmosphere is sustained by the imagination for crime that the fragile self develops.

83
Meanwhile, on the other side, it is a town composed of white buildings, a watering place, a seaside resort in summer. Out there, in the middle of the beach, in the shade of the lime trees, the band will play soon in the bandstand, for the people walking by or sitting around. In a room, probably fairly high up, overlooking the main avenue, an unknown woman standing beside me (but it is her), dressed in black, is speaking to me in insistent whispers.

47

Error, optical illusion, provides the material out of which truth must emerge, as evolution must emerge out of the regression and elimination of many species.

But *emerge* is as vague a word as the language possesses for so crucial a process, biological, moral or esthetic. Emerge how?

80

Listen, do you want to make an effort or don't you? You were so stupid the last time. Don't you see how beautiful this moment could be? Look at the sky, look at the color of the sun on the carpet. I've got my green dress on and my face isn't made up, I'm quite pale. Go back, go and sit in the shadow; you understand what you have to do? Come on! How stupid you are! Speak to me!

69

She tried to free herself. No, no, I know that tone of voice. You're going to treat me to another of those nonsensical outbursts. When you put on that tone of voice and face, I know that you're going to prove that your eye is shaped like a striped super-mullet, or that your mouth looks like the figure three on its side. No, no, I can't stand that.

22

Very often the novel writes about contracts but dreams of transgressions, and in reading it, the dream tends to emerge more powerfully.

16

You've been trying to find things out?

Without success; there's probably nothing to be found out.

52
How did she find out?
Madame Saphir put her on the track.
Who?
Madame Saphir, the clairvoyant in the rue Taine. She
set up shop there about six months ago and all the old girls
in the district go and consult her. Haven't *you* been?
I'm not an old girl, said Julia.

79
Don't complain about improbability. What is going to follow
is false and no one is bound to accept it as gospel truth.
Truth is not my strong point. "But one has to lie in order to
be true." And even go beyond. What truth do I want to talk
about? If it is really true that I am a prisoner who plays
(who plays for himself) scenes of the inner life, you will
require nothing other than a game.

53
Like Flaubert, too, that brown table to the left with a pen-
knife-cut in it (another Bovary), that carefully unconscious
but fundamentally so naive and almost sentimental table, is
yourself. And if you make use of the table, if you cannot
leave it alone, why should I not make use of the lie?

60
And you complain of my conduct! And you are surprised by
my eagerness to avoid you! Ah! Rather blame my indul-
gence, rather be surprised that I did not leave at the
moment you arrived. I ought perhaps to have done so; and
you will compel me to this violent but necessary course if
you do not cease your offensive pursuit.

85

It is, it should be made quite clear, not a dream but a day-dream; Flaubert says, Curiously enough, that, while Charles dozed off beside her, Emma "was awake in a very different dreamland." In view of this, one cannot fail to be surprised by the clarity and precision of certain details, like the stork's nests on the spiky steeples, the flagstones that slowed them down to a foot-pace, the red bodices, the spray from the fountains, the pyramid of fruits, the brown nets, etc.

79

The man with a good memory does not remember anything because he does not forget anything. His memory is uniform, a creature of routine, at once a condition and function of his impeccable habit, an instrument of reference instead of an instrument of discovery. The paean of his memory: "I remember as well as I remember yesterday. . ." is also its epitaph, and gives the precise expression of its value. He cannot *remember* yesterday anymore than he can remember tomorrow.

38

What do you want, he asked with a cruel smile. I guessed what he was thinking, and that my request had had no other meaning for him. I blurted out the first thing that came into my head.

46

The only aspect I can remember of this affair which, though banal, played a decisive part in my life, was the exquisite presentiment I then had of nothingness. It all took place in a hotel room in Lyon, the most inhospitable town in France.

79

Breathe in, breathe out. Breathe naturally. Imagine that your arm has grown heavy, very heavy. Think: My right arm is very limp and heavy. My left arm is limp and very heavy. My arm is very heavy. Imagine that your head is falling back a little. Keep your eyes tight shut. Imagine that your shoulders are light. My shoulders are so light. Imagine that your right leg is heavy. Think, I'm very relaxed and my leg is very heavy.

3
But who? Who?

66
She says: there's no reason why you should have acted differently, you know, I quite understand.
He says: so much the better. Let's go on, the other moves will be just as easy, it's a pretty banal inquiry.
She says: I believe you, absolutely banal, still, let's go on. I can give you a few more details.
He says: O.K., then it'll help things move on.

42
The telephone didn't ring.
It's a good fifteen minutes since the explosion. It wasn't in the old city then. But in the industrial sections, or farther north.
Marietti is still sleeping. Perez looks completely asleep. Three short explosions, brutally shattering the silence. . .

13
What the devil is this, he muttered, are you going to be difficult?

96
Nowadays, one no longer says: You've got a soul and you must save it, but: You've got a sexual nature, and you must find how to use it well.

You've got an unconscious, and you must learn how to liberate it.

You've got a body and you must learn how to enjoy it.

You've got a libido, and you must learn how to spend it, etc. This compulsion toward liquidity, flow, and an accelerated circulation of what is psychic, sexual, or pertaining to the body is the exact replica of the force which rules the market value.

71

What is the meaning of this door? Its presence brings to mind some ignoble police stake-out, the pursuit of a sentimental assassin undone by the weakness of the flesh who finds himself hunted at daybreak in this labyrinth of desire where he had come for asylum; hand on beating heart, standing nervously on tip-toe, the ill-starred hero can still hear the unconscious sighs of pleasure behind other doors.

51

Coup with Safia Zugairah (Little Sophie)—I stain the divan. She is very corrupt and writhing, extremely voluptuous. But the best was the second copulation with Kuchuk. Effects of her necklace between my teeth. Her cunt felt like rolls of velvet as she made me come. I felt like a tiger.

48

We have no difficulty in recognizing the interplay and mutual illumination of two worlds in this example, but the challenge is more severe when it is not clear who is speaking, where the ordering of the parts is less controlled or where there are more than two parts.

48

The oriental woman is an occasion and an opportunity for Flaubert's musing; he is entranced by her self-sufficiency, by her emotional carelessness, and also by what, lying next to him, she allows him to think. Less a woman than a display of impressive but verbally inexpressive femininity.

160

The man utters a hoarse sound. O. says Ahahaha, then quickly pulls her thighs up against her body, the knees almost touching her shoulders while her hand which has been clutching the yellow head of hair releases it, the arm straightening, the hand moving down the length of the body around the bent thigh, the buttock reaching the base of the member thrust deep within her, sticky now with the semen which dribbles irregularly from her cunt, flowing down between her own buttocks. Despite the uninterrupted back-and-forth movement of the penis, she gets a grip on it and in a moment when the man withdraws she pulls back the skin so as to release the glans. When the latter thrusts into her again her throat emits the same strangled cry, then she begins jabbering a series of broken words. One of the bedsprings creaks faintly. Someone is walking in the corridor outside. O. says Shshshsh! and becomes motionless.

64

He asked me if I had felt any sadness that day. The question caught me by surprise and it seemed to me that I would have been very embarrassed if I'd had to ask it. Nevertheless I answered that I had pretty much lost the habit of analyzing myself and that it was hard for me to tell him what he wanted to know.

15

When she got home she spent two hours on her sofa crying from nervous exhaustion.

95

Did he understand women at all? I often doubted it. We quarrelled, I remember, over that Nilotic whore of his,

Kuchuk Hanem. Gustav kept notes during his travels. I
asked if I could read them. He refused; I asked again; and
so on. Finally he let me. They are not. . . pleasant, those
pages. What Gustav found enchanting about the East I
found degrading. A courtesan, an expensive courtesan, who
drenches herself in sandalwood oil to cover the nauseating
stench of the bedbugs with which she is infested. Is that
uplifting, I ask, is it beautiful?

82

The sound of the city is so near, so close, you can hear it
brushing against the wood of the shutters. It sounds as if
they're all going through the rooms. I caress his body amid
the sound, the passer-by. The sea, the immensity, gathering, receding, returning.

I asked him to do it again and again. Do it to me. And he
did, did it in the unctuousness of blood. And it really was
unto death. It has been unto death.

109

The last two days Victor has hardly shown his face, has
said neither good-morning nor good-evening, has looked
glum, has not answered when spoken to, and has walked by
you without seeing you. I am indeed very silly to be concerned about it.

23 January

But I should like to know whether he would act in this unci-
vil manner and show the same disregard for anyone whatsoever, or whether, as I fear, this reveals a particular hostility
to me. To be sure, he may not like feeling constantly ob-
served and judged by me, and judged very severely. I am
the only one to stand up to him.

83

. . . If I weren't living outside my own times this way, in
history the way other people live in religion, I could

resuscitate, and by inadequate fragments, only the historical past, the only one that *can* be known because it's the only one worthy to be preserved. Despite the chroniclers who have here and there put down a few chance details, and despite the often unpublished documents that I discover or collect, the essentials of this daily life of *past* Parisians would escape me.

73
    Charlotte: If I asked you what your good qualities were, what would you say?
    Robert: My good qualities? Why not my faults?
    Charlotte: No. It's your good qualities I'm interested in.
    Robert: Intelligence. Distrustfulness.
    Charlotte: Is distrustfulness a quality?
    Robert: Yes.
    Charlotte: Is that all?
    Robert: Sincerity. . .
    Charlotte: What about loving me?
    Robert: Oh yes, that's a quality. And you, what would you say your qualities are?
    Charlotte: Never think twice about anything.

5
    What is optimism? asked Cacambo. .

80
The museum bookshop also has on display my speech about the preservation of the monuments of Nubia, and big photographs of the work in progress. I remember the rounded black rocks of Aswan reflected in the Styx-colored Nile. They had probably not changed a great deal since the time when the young Flaubert caught syphilis there from a girl whose name, Kutchek Hanem, dazzled him as though it were the Queen of Sheba. I believe it stands for "Little Lady."

110

Ethel was closeted on a balcony (she did look pretty wise, I
must admit, in an unexpected schoolmistressly way), and
one by one her clients disappeared for consultations, taking
their coffee cups with them—her divinatory system made
use of the coffee grounds. In the meantime the rest of us
chatted, and a very suggestive chat I found it. Did we know
that G was almost certainly going to St. Tropez with A?
Was it really true that B was getting Omani money for his
new hotel? Had we tried the chopped liver at the Hilton?
What about F selling that awful house of his for a quarter of
a million?

102

On the contrary, they wanted to hear her screams; and the
sooner the better. The pride she mustered to resist and
remain silent did not long endure: they even heard her beg
them to untie her, to stop for a second, just for a second. So
frantically did she writhe, trying to escape the bite of the
lashes, that she turned almost completely around, on the
near side of the pole, for the chain which held was long and,
although quite solid, fairly slack. As a result, her belly and
the front of her thighs were almost as marked as her back-
side.

95

You know that he didn't undress
I saw them from the garden once they hadn't pulled the
curtains as I was passing I saw them mind you it may have
been the only time he didn't undress I was intrigued I
stayed there, at moments like that people aren't so aware of
things
What did you see
What I told you
Give details
It's not the sort of things you can talk about

Give details you must
Oh well he was sitting on the divan and she was doing it
to him just like that

19
Later the same day He arrived just in time—so I thought—to
get me out of my difficulties.

76
We just stood there for quite a long time, until one of them
shattered the windshield with the handle of a sturdy knife,
then all the windows, and then two others set about kicking
in the doors; others attacked the lights and the tires and
anything else they could find, the whole thing in the most
eerie silence. I stood there watching my car being de-
stroyed, neither doing anything or saying anything, for a
good while.

98
We read a text (of pleasure) the way a fly buzzes around a
room: with sullen, deceptively decisive turns, fervent and
futile: ideology passes over the text and its reading like the
blush over a face (in love, some take erotic pleasure in this
coloring); every writer of pleasure has these idiotic blushes
(Balzac, Zola, Flaubert, Proust: only Mallarmé, perhaps is
the master of his skin): in the text of pleasure, the opposing
forces are no longer repressed but in a state of becoming:
nothing is really antagonistic, everything is plural. I pass
lightly through the reactionary darkness.

44
She answered me, from the seaside resort where she was
staying, by a postcard signed by her first name spelled back-
ward. I solved the riddle quickly enough, and again I was
pleased, for it seemed that I was not being forgotten despite
my solitude.

64

During this little expedition there occurred a painful incident between Flaubert and me, the only one during the entire trip: we did not speak to each other for forty-eight hours. It was both unpleasant and comical, for in this case Flaubert obeyed one of those irresistible impulses that sometimes overcome him. Besides, in the desert one is hypersensitive, as the story will show.

36

Gustav was clearly less disturbed over the arrival of the Prussians than over the deaths of an alarming number of his ideal readers. It seemed to him that no one was left for whom to write.

98

No! he said. It's not you that disgusts me, it's everything. I don't want anything. . . You can't hold that against me. . .

What's that you say? Say it again! Me. . . everything? She was trying to understand. Me everything? Don't talk Chinese!. . . Tell me in French, in front of these people. Why do I disgust you now? Don't you get a hard-on like everybody else, you big pig, when you make love? Oh, so you don't get a hard-on, is that it?. . . Out with it!. . . In front of these people. Tell us you don't get a hard-on!

61

But the truth is elsewhere. The "surface" of the body is not comparable to a stage curtain or cinema screen or a painter's canvas. It is full of holes, or rather, the holes are part of the skin; skin involutes by hollowing out the so-called "inside" (point of view of the theater), which is just as external as the "outside."

112
Because of this, all the works he undertakes are extrava-
gant; in each one he is shattered by "horrifying" difficulties;
each time he promises himself that the next one will be
easy, happy, more suited to his talent, and each time he
chooses the only one he cannot write: "I must be absolutely
mad to undertake a book like this one. . . I must be crazy
and completely out of my mind to undertake such a book!
I'm afraid that in its very conception it is radically impossible. . . What terror! I feel as though I am about to embark
on a very long voyage towards unknown regions, and that I
won't be coming back."

173
I was recently told a story that was so stupid, so melan-
choly, and so moving; a man comes into a hotel one day and
asks to rent a room. He is shown up to number 35. As he
comes down a few minutes later and leaves the key at the
desk, he says: Excuse me, I have no memory at all. If you
please, each time I come in, I'll tell you my name: Monsieur
Delouit. And each time you'll tell me the number of my
room. —Very well Monsieur. Soon afterwards he returns,
and as he passes the desk says: Monsieur Delouit.
—Number 35, Monsieur. Thank you. A few minutes later,
a man extraordinarily upset, his clothes covered with mud,
bleeding, his face almost not a face at all, appears at the
desk: Monsieur Delouit. What do you mean, Monsieur
Delouit. Don't try to put one over us! Monsieur Delouit has
gone upstairs! I'm sorry, it's me. . . I've just fallen out of
the window. What's the number of my room please?

66
    Do you know, this is the first time I've ever liked being in
a hotel.
    What I usually dislike about hotels is that there might be
hidden microphones.

Yes, behind the pictures or lamps.
Yes, I always feel someone's listening to what I say.
There wouldn't be much point.
What, in listening to what people say?
Yes.
Yes, but it bothers me all the same.
I—

28
I'm quite happy that you should have such an opinion of
me. By God, I'm in great danger from you, that I'm sure of.
And so am I.

84
The bedroom window—the one nearest the hallway—opens
outward. The upper part of A. . .'s body is framed within it.
She says "Hello" in the playful tone of someone who has
slept well and awakened in a good mood; or of someone who
prefers not to show what she is thinking about—if anything—and always flashes the same smile, on principle: the
same smile, which can be interpreted as derision just as well
as affection, or the total absence of any feeling whatever.

20
Please come to the point and tell me what you expected from
me and how I disappointed you, I interjected.

8
Then, insiduously, illusion began to plant its snares.

97
We have admired this remark (Flaubert's, Madame Bovary,
c'est moi) for more than a hundred years. We also admire
the tears Flaubert shed when he had to let Madame Bovary
die, and the crystal clear calculation of his wonderful novel,
which he was able to write despite his tears; and we should

not and will not stop admiring him. But Flaubert was not
Madame Bovary; we cannot completely ignore that fact in
the end, despite all our good will and what we know of the
secret relationship between an author and a figure created
by art.

40
Sartre has indeed succeeded in showing how Flaubert fetish-
ized his own imaginary femininity while simultaneously
sharing his period's hostility toward real women, participat-
ing in a pattern of the imagination and of behavior all too
common in the history of modernism.

142
"Your husband is adorable. You know how fond I am of him:
like a son. And, in reality, he's fond of me, I know it, he's so
sweet; he's so young, so charming, but it must be admitted
that he is not exactly the husband your father and I should
have wished for. He's not quite mature enough. . . I'm not
speaking of his age. . . It's a question of temperament. Your
father was mature when he was twenty-five. . ." Only look
out. Her little girl withdraws slightly, she's about to take
cover in one of her stubborn silences which it takes any
amount of trouble to get her out of . . . "It isn't the question

of his position, you know that. Other parents than ourselves
would perhaps have taken it with bad grace, but you know
very well that, for us, that hasn't mattered. . ."

46
These negotiations had taken a great deal of time and trouble. The lesser deals which provided me with my day-to-day
living had suffered in consequence; I hoped nevertheless to
resell the clip for a million francs and so retrieve the situation in good time.

61
The road to honor is closed to him.
Why so, I asked.
We have a rule of thumb in France, he replied, and that is
never to promote officers whose patience has languished in
subordinate posts. We think of them as men whose minds
have shrunken into details, and through the habit of little
things, have become incapable of greater ones.

28
                                        Wednesday, March 14. In town I
am a bad reader, constantly backing away from what is in
front of me, out of either hatred, refusal or bad faith.

72
He turned away while I fixed my skirt, went to get my
handbag, gave it back to me, and offered me a glass of
cognac. But I slapped him. Then he snatched away my
skirt again, stepped on it, put his hands back in his pockets,
and without flinching, received another slap; and with that I
couldn't stop until I lost consciousness. . . Actually, what
could a woman do in such a situation?

14
I shall now endeavor to describe what he shall perhaps see
from the rooftop.

117
Or again in the perfume department. A low glass counter.
The sales girl, pink blouse high heels too much make-up.
The young woman says something, points with her index
finger to a shelf, then to her chin or to her neck. The sales
girl turns around, takes two or three steps towards the
shelf, takes down a pale thin cardboard box, turns around
again to the young woman who has just spoken to her
again, nods her head, in profile, on her left lower down takes

one, a small square box, comes back to the counter, puts the two articles on the glass of the counter. Bright blue eyes. Mouth. She waits. Expressionless then more alert.

38
He set off for the village. The others hadn't bothered to wait for him. The gates slammed behind him with a resounding clang. A gust of wind had probably caught them. It went on whistling between the bars.

6
Let's go and follow your mistake.

14
But when at last his wishes were granted, he suffered immediate and immeasurable disappointment.

43
His verdict on *Swann* was reported to the author: "It beats Flaubert hollow!"; and in the spring of 1916, on leave in Bardac's Paris flat, Morand was woken by a night-visitor who proclaimed, 'in a ceremonious, bleating voice',: "I am Marcel Proust."

12
Ah my boy, the country is the country, and Paris is Paris.

101
    I would like to make you happy.
    Frederic suspected that Mme. Arnoux had come to offer herself to him; and he was repossessed by a desire stronger than ever, furious, raging. However, he sensed something inexpressible, a repulsion, as if the fear of incest. Another fear stopped him, that of feeling disgust afterward. More-

over, what a nuisance it would be! and at once from pru-
dence, and in order not to degrade his ideal, he turned on his
heel and began to roll a cigarette.
     She looked at him in wonder.
     How fine you are! There's no one like you, no one!

78
When his sentences ran dry, Flaubert flung himself on his
divan: he called this his "marinade." If the thing reverber-
ates too powerfully, it makes such a din in my body that I
must halt any occupation; I stretch out on my bed and give
in without a struggle to the "inner storm"; contrary to the
Zen monk who empties himself of his images, I let myself be
filled by them, I indulge in their bitterness to the full.

6
     About time too. I'm worn out.

23
Rosi: "It just goes to prove, Alice, that our struggles are far
from being over—in fact, they are just beginning for real..."

54
A Mandarin fell in love with a courtesan. "I shall be yours,"
she told him, "when you have spent a hundred nights waiting for me, sitting on a stool, in my garden, beneath my
window." But on the ninety-ninth night, the Mandarin stood
up, put his stool under his arm, and went away.

10
You are right. I must have been in the clouds.

READING
KAFKA
IN GERMAN

50
After we had been talking for a little less than two hours, he made it clear he didn't want to say more: I am nearly eighty years old, and . . . I don't want to have anything more to do with that era . . . I don't want to think about it any more.

62
But isn't there a need to be more precise? Nothing happened to everyday language, whether it was German, English, French or Russian, and one can continue to sing about the butterflies as if nothing happened. But there it is: It is no longer a matter of butterflies or flowers, and, one ascertains it, the inadequacy grows between the language and certain events.

11
A hotel; the market-place; and the Town Hall was facing him.

81

The members of the student corps all wore gaily colored
caps, gaily colored sashes, and those walking in the middle
each carried a colored flag that hung down heavy and silken.
There were seven or eight ranks of three students in succession, and the group as a whole was the most gaily colored I
had ever seen. The faces of the students were very solemn,
and they all stared straight ahead without blinking, appar-
ently at some very remote and fascinating goal.

83

Things that were in the shopwindow. A basket of German
Jagdwurst, some in a pile others lying higgledy-piggledy, a
basket of egg crackers, a basket of tinned Hamburgers, a
basket of black-currant wine some bottles standing some
lying, a basket of pickled gherkins in jars some whole some
sliced, a basket of washing-up brushes in various colors, a
basket of Pfälzer white wine with all the bottles upright,
plus meatballs for soup, tinned milk, eggs in boxes, two
cardboard boxes containing electric dryers.

89

First of all, my inquiry is not concerned with the physiology
of aging. What medicine has to say on this subject doesn't
amount to much. Its current formula is that aging is not a
process of wear-and-tear but an adaptation, and I must say
this doesn't convey much to me. It goes on, as I have discovered from its journals, to deplore the lack of unpreju-
diced, systematic psychological examinations of old people
who are not in psychiatric clinics. I don't know how many
of you will also deplore this.

74

Before long we were again talking and joking about indifferent subjects; but when I went to him, and told him that he
should   have   my   objection   in   writing   for   a   closer

examination, and that the only reason that he did not agree with me lay in the clumsiness of my verbal statement, he could not help, with a half-laugh and half-sneer, throwing in my teeth at the very doorway something about heretics and heresy.

84
He often speaks of his bad memory, but in reality nothing escapes him. The acuteness of his memory is reflected in the way he corrects and completes Felice's imprecise memories of earlier years. It is a fact, all the same, that he cannot always freely recall his memories. His obduracy keeps them out of his reach; he cannot like other writers, play with his memories irresponsibly. This obduracy follows its own stringent laws—one might say that it helps him husband his defensive forces.

53
The wall is hard to find on a city map in West Berlin. Only a dotted band, delicate pink, divides the city. On a city map in East Berlin, the world ends at the Wall. Beyond the black-bordered, finger-thick dividing line identified in the key as the state border, untenanted geography sets in.

36
Why didn't I tell him that it was I who had read his diary? No, not yet. Not there and then, in front of everybody. I couldn't. I'd be too ashamed. Later, yes, but not yet.

49
Suddenly I had to think of him. Say a picture of him suddenly floated before me. Did I know it was a picture of him, N? I did not tell myself it was. What did its being of him consist in then? Perhaps what I later said or did.

116

We attach ourselves to certain people, then suddenly we hate them and let go. We run after them for years, begging for their affection, I thought, and when once we have their affection we no longer want it. We flee from them and they catch up with us and seize hold of us, and we submit to them and all their dictates, I thought, surrendering to them until we either die or break loose. We flee from them and they catch up with us and crush us to death. Or else we avoid them from the beginning and succeed in avoiding them all our lives, I thought. Or we walk into their trap and suffocate. Or we escape from them and start running them down, slandering them and spreading lies about them, I thought, in order to save ourselves, slandering them wherever we can in order to save ourselves, running away from them for dear life and accusing them everywhere of having *us* on their conscience.

68

Sometimes I sit there exuding silence. And there I sit, in that silence. Like under a glass cover. Then, ladies and gentlemen, it gets to me. Depression, I mean, the resentful, self-devouring kind. Because now I'm worth no more than something you throw at the wall to smash it so completely that you can't tell from the pieces what it was or what it was meant to be.

46

    Once he asked her: Do you still believe that everything is going to turn out all right.
    Are you talking about yourself?
    I'm not just talking about myself, but I am talking about myself as well.
    What else then?
    I mean everything else.
    What else? Life?

97

The waiter had peered through the veranda and condescended to take an order. Gaudy rowboats rocked at the breakwater in front of the restaurant. You always made a point of showing me that I didn't have the least claim on you, said Anna. Now you don't bother. You say nothing, and I ask nothing of you. I've thought about it all this time and I've concluded you wanted to end it back then. I often had the impression that I'd become a burden to you. I was surprised that what I told you affected you so deeply.

77

We often encounter in everyday life something which, when we encounter it in art, we are accustomed to attribute to the poet's artistry: when the chief characters are absent or concealed, or lapse into inactivity, their place is at once taken by a second or third character who has hardly been noticed before, and when this character then comes fully into his own he seems just as worthy of our attention and sympathy and even our praise.

66

The intellectual approach is a compound of Jewishness and the Stefan George brand of Germanic thinking. It is a happy mixture, and may be the only way to get to the heart of things these days. But the Germanic element, which is usually insufferable when it speaks on its own behalf, is treated here with too much deference, at least in view of its present-day behavior.

68

All of Europe is sweltering in this heat wave. Thirty degrees Celsius in the shade, mid-June, mackerel skies, day after day the same thing. It promises to be a summer the like of which comes only once a century. At seven in the morning the first sprinkler truck passes under his window. He

awakens in the same gloomy spirits in which he dropped off
the night before.

34
Had his duties not been comparatively simple and he himself not virtually become over the years an almost mechani-
cal part of the service he could not in all conscience have
continued in his duties.

51
This picture, not to call it an idea, possessed all our heads,
companionably side by side with another: the belief that we
were forced into war, that sacred necessity called us to take
our weapons—those well polished weapons whose readiness
and excellence always induced a secret temptation to test
them.

88
I began to speak, and spoke about two and a half hours and
my feeling told me after the first half hour that the meeting
would be a great success. Contact with all these thousands
of individuals had been established. After the first hour the
applause began to interrupt me in greater and greater spon-
taneous outbursts, ebbing off after two hours into that solemn stillness which I have later experienced so very often in
this hall, and which will remain unforgettable to every single member of this audience.

11
I am not a theoretician, as I believe to have demonstrated.

87
The brutal exhibition of the severed ears had shocked me.
But it was inevitable as motif. Wasn't it necessarily the
result of a perfection of technique to whose initial intoxica-
tion it had put an end. Had there been in any period in the

history of the world as many mutilated bodies, as many severed limbs as in ours? Mankind has waged war since the world began, but I can't remember one single example in the entire *Iliad* where the loss of an arm or leg is reported.

5
Yes, he had lost face.

61
The children are the first to congratulate me. They stand up straight and pipe up their poems and hand over their gifts and flowers. Wonderfully sweet! Together we all watch the film that Heinz made with the children; brings on laughters and tears, it is so beautiful. Then we wander through our new house, which is tremendous fun for the children.

48
He had money, power, growing fame, and popularity; a charming, gracious, and cultured wife; an expanding industrial and commercial conglomeration of twenty-three companies with gross revenues of about $200 million; luxurious homes in Hamburg and Düsseldorf, and a chalet, complete with its own mountain, in the Bavarian Alps.

69
The woman: I suddenly had an illumination—another word she had to laugh at—that you were going away, that you were leaving me. Yes, that's it. Go away Bruno. Leave me.

After a while Bruno nodded slowly, raised his arms in a gesture of helplessness, and asked: For good?

The woman: I don't know. All I know is that you'll go away and leave me. They stood silent.

50
The resort town is a disappointment, too. Several rows of ugly concrete buildings line the beach for miles on end, a

sprawling city that lives entirely off the tourist trade and
consists of nothing but hotels and shops. It's hard to imagine
that real people lived here thirty years ago.

106
I TRY ON STORIES LIKE CLOTHES
More and more often some memory comes along and
shocks me. Usually those memories are not shocking in
themselves, little things not worth telling in the kitchen or
as a passenger in a car. What shocks me is rather the discovery that I have been concealing my life from myself. I
have been serving up stories to some sort of public, and in
these stories, I know, I have laid myself bare—to the point
of non-recognition. I live, not with my own story, but just
with those parts of it that I have been able to put to literary
use.

22
On reading it, Simrock was amused by the expression
"revolutionary patience": his own ear told him that it should
be "revolutionary impatience."

83
The Trial contains vivid descriptions of everyday urban life.
Readers usually overlook them because of the anxiety
aroused by Joseph K.'s abstract struggle with the court, but
they are important because they posit the existence of a real
community in the world and of this novel. (One of Kafka's
largely unrecognized talents is his ability to show ordinary
people at their day-to-day living, even if these scenes are
susceptible of being interpreted in the light of Lefebvre's
concept of "terrorism and everyday life.")

53
A gentleman enters.
It's me, he says.

Try again, we call out.
He enters anew.
Here I am, he says.
That's not much better, we call.
Again he enters the room.
I'm the one, he says.
A bad beginning, we call.
He enters again.
Hello, he calls. He waves.
Please don't, we say.

40
The phenomenological theory of art lays full stress on the idea that, in considering a literary text, one must take into account not only the actual text but also, in equal measure, the actions involved in responding to that text.

52
Despite its misuse by the National Socialists, we cannot deny that the idea of art being bound to a people involves a real insight. A genuine artistic creation stands within a particular community, and such a community is always distinguishable from the cultured society that is informed and terrorized by art criticism.

89
Why would a man like Kafka decide that if he had to fall short of his destiny, being a writer was the only way to fall short of it? Perhaps this is an unintelligible enigma, but if it is, the source of the mystery is literature's right to affix a negative or positive sign indiscriminately to each of its moments and each of its results. A strange right—one linked to the question of ambiguity in general. Why is there ambiguity in the world? Ambiguity is its own answer.

14
There is nothing more memorable than the fervor with which Kafka emphasized his failure.

60
The cloakroom lady hung my coat in a dumbwaiter and let it descend into the basement, and I stepped into the cafe. The geography was finally right for me: The huge windows, where I looked for a table, were in the direct firing line of one of the tanks that had come straight at me too.
    I was in Prague.

26
When living in Prague, the city where Joseph K. fought for his life, *The Trial* was too close to home for me to recognize its meaning.

35
The only way to escape, it seemed, was to tear himself free from the whole relationship, from "all that sort of thing." And this was the direction in which his thoughts now burrowed and probed.

73
Kafka's feelings about his work are extreme, but they at least illustrate the type of enterprise a writer engages in. The text's condemnation is based on the fact that so far as the writer is concerned *all* questions—about his life, his work, his mind—are referable to it, are surveyed from its viewpoint. Everything he writes, whether letters, notes, sketches, or riddles, bears upon it the mark of responsibility to the text.

37
Something imponderable. A prognostic. An illusion. Like what happens when a magnet lets the iron filings go and

they tumble together again. . . Or when a tension has slackened. . . Or when an orchestra begins to play out of tune. . . .

26
But the key fact about Kafka is that he was possessed of a fearful premonition, that he saw, to the point of exact detail, the horror gathering.

67
Yes, yes, he said thoughtfully, and without a trace of shame. He even smiled. All kinds of stories made the rounds, and are still making the rounds, and much of what people say is exaggerated. But it's true we had to be pretty tough on the suspects when an 'intensive interrogation' was ordered. I often had to clench my teeth to make myself go through with it.

109
After this experience I resolved in similar cases to go at once straight to facts. I noticed how simple they were and what a relief compared with conjectures. As if I had not known that all our insights are added later, balances, nothing more. Right afterwards a new page begins with something entirely different, nothing carried forward. Of what help in the present case were the few facts, which it was child's play to establish? I shall relate them immediately, when I have told what concerns me at the moment: that these facts tended rather to make my situation, which (as I now admit) was really difficult, still more embarrassing.

49
On 6 November 1942 Heinrich Himmler had given his support to a plan to establish a collection of Jewish skulls and skeletons at the Reich Anatomical Institute in Strasbourg, near Natzweiler, where they were measured, weighed and

gassed, and their corpses sent on to the Anatomical Institue in Strasbourg.

16
But let's go back to the beginning of our story, which still hasn't got very far.

79
They clinked steins, they drank up, they set the steins back on the table, they waited for a refill. The Oberländer band was playing. They were old gentlemen in short leather pants that showed their hairy, reddened knees. The band played glowworm, it played once-a-boy-a-girl-did-see, and everyone in the hall sang along, they linked arms, they stood up, they got up on beer benches, they raised their steins and bellowed, each syllable drawn out long and with feeling, rose-upon-the-hill-side.

15
    Two men were talking.
    Your estimate?
    With tiles?
    Of course, with green tiles.
    Forty thousand.

83
Major Castille recalls that the tour "was like being in a magician's cave." There were two tunnels running parallel to each other for slightly more than a mile into the mountainside. Here V-1 and V-2 parts were arranged in orderly rows. Cross tunnels were filled with precision machinery and tools. Telephone, ventilating, and lighting systems were still in operation. The huge subterranean complex had not been damaged and appeared to have been abandoned in perfect working order by its German guards and technicians.

9
After a week one feels quite at home here.

102
I climb up to the fortress instead of down, then along the chain of hills to the Lauterbach Valley. Black Forest farms come into view without warning. I have probably made several wrong decisions in a row concerning my route, and in retrospect, this has led me to the proper course. What is really bad is that after acknowledging a wrong decision, I don't have the nerve to turn back, since I would rather correct myself with another wrong decision. But I am following a direct imaginary line anyway, which is, however, not always possible, and so the deviations are not great. . .

43
If I turned my head a bit I could see it more clearly, but still, couldn't tell for certain, what, if I looked at it straight it was there at one moment, gone the next, but it was something white all the time.

44
And there is the murky sadness of the flats, low clouds in the west, gusts of wind curling the water in the runnels and pools, and causing the sea birds' feathers to bristle; in the distance there is the faint hum of an airplane.

5
Does everyone think like you?

74
For in our country everything is geared to growth. We're never satisfied. For us enough is never enough. We always want more. If it's on paper we convert it into reality. Even in our dreams we are productive. We do everything that's feasible. And to our minds everything thinkable is feasible.

To be German is to make the impossible possible. Has there ever been a German who, after recognizing the impossible, accepted its impossibility?

36

If there is no transcendence beyond the abyss, the abyss must be inspected further. The descent deeper into the abyss must take place; in a word, the abyss must be *sub-scended*, penetrated to its perceivable depths.

42

Through the Heisenbergs or von Brauns, with Furtwängler's music and Heidegger's and Benn's and Hauptmann's language, how would we be today, at the victory celebration in Speer's Berlin? The whole world the way it was for a moment at the Olympic games.

47

Ignore, overlook, neglect, deny, unlearn, obliterate, forget. According to recent discoveries, the changeover of experiences from short-term to long-term memory supposedly takes place at night, through dreams. You imagine a nation of sleepers, a people whose dreaming brains are complying with the given command: Cancel cancel cancel.

28

I can still see her face as the train moved off; pale under its brown light, like a blossom, smiling. The hunt for her is on once more.

36

One reason Kafka's writing gives such difficulty, when it seems so limpid, is that his spacing is in multiples. What seems foreground becomes, by receding, background, and vice versa; as if a given "picture" had actual movement.

97
For world and thing do not subsist alongside one another.
They penetrate each other. Thus the two traverse a middle.
In it, they are one. Thus at one they are intimate. The middle of the two is intimacy—in latin, *inter*. The correspond-
ing German word is *unter*, the English *inter*-. The intimacy
of a world and thing is not a fusion. Intimacy obtains only
where the intimate—world and thing—divides itself cleanly
and remains separated. In the midst of the two, in the between of the world and thing, in their *inter*, division prevails:
a *dif-ference*.

51
If one discusses these figures with well-informed members of
the Bundestag or Federal adminstrators, one can often hear
this objection: Such figures have no really convincing effect
on us. We would like to have particular well-founded scien-
tific projects put before us, but not these general considera-
tions, which are difficult to check.

19
Concrete demands can now cheerfully be made. There is no
danger that they may be implemented with disagreeable
consequences.

7
Should one speak out or be silent?

52
It was still in the afternoon when he stopped at a gas sta-
tion and tried to call the bar in West Berlin. He dialed four
figures to West Berlin, six figures across the city to a coin
telephone by which, he now assumed, Beate must be standing. Is she there? he said.

25
We have learned, in effect that meaning in history, memory
of the past, and the writing of history are by no means to be
equated.

29
    I thought you had decided to stand me up, she said as he
sat down.
    Why?
    You still owe me an answer. Or have you already forgot-
ten my question?

50
And then there was her deep voice. Once I woke her up in
the middle of the night, and when she woke with a start, I
said, Say something!
    You idiot, she said, and fell asleep smiling. But I heard
her voice, I had heard that wonderful contralto voice.

74
Who was really close to him? If we believed the claims of
surviving contemporaries, there would be a sizable list. For
his death provoked many people to say something about
him; during his lifetime his anomalous conduct may have
made some of them uneasy. They had been helpless in the
face of his eccentric behavior, which in his last years was at
times puzzling and unpredictable, and, in his last months,
occasionally insufferable.

42
Say something! Erika begged, in a strangled voice, while we
stumbled side by side through the maze of flower-beds and
bushes. If you don't talk, I'll fall again. . . oh! Into the bot-
tomless. . . into the big black hole. . . Why don't you say
something?

75
Travelling through the town where she lived I saw her name on a playbill. I called on her in her dressing room. The play was over; she had appeared in her mask, her costume as queen. Attired in crinoline, with a leaf-entwined shepherd's crook in her hand, a high powdered wig on her head, a large gold-glittering ornament about her neck, her mouth and eyes coarsely outlined, she turned towards me in slow incredulous recognition.

113
How can we enter into Kafka's work? This work is a rhizome, a burrow. The castle has multiple entrances whose rules of usage and whose locations aren't very well known. The hotel in *Amerika* has innumerable main doors and side doors that innumerable guards watch over; it even has entrances and exits without doors. Yet it might seem that the burrow in the story of that name has only one entrance; the most the animal can do is dream of a second entrance that would serve only for surveillance. But this is a trap arranged by the animal and by Kafka himself; the whole description of the burrow functions to trick the enemy.

91
To this prestigious edifice, in which beauty and luxury are associated with the memory of absolute power and archaic customs, the German *Schloss* adds one more important characteristic that is not perceptible in the English castle (or the French *château)*, since it evokes not only the building but also its enclosed character *(Schloss* also means "lock" and is related to several verbs expressing the idea of closure), so that all the moral, social, spiritual, and aesthetic qualities implicit in the image appear automatically as values defended from within, literally "walled around."

31

In brief we were given the image of a manorial castle with an administrative staff out of proportion to its modest estate, and with corrupt officials—just as Kafka described it.

93

He estimated that around one million neurotics, as well as those who were suffering from psychosomatic illnesses, were in need of care in West Germany at the time, and there were only about 200 practitioners of *grosse* psychotherapy in the whole country. He remarked that any potential danger that lay therapists, supervised by a physician, might overlook an organic illness or incipient psychosis was far outweighed by what he saw as the reality of the medical profession's continued undervaluation of the effects of the unconscious on the genesis and persistence of physical ailments.

77

'Alas,' said the mouse, 'the world is growing smaller every day. At first it was so big that I was afraid, I ran on and was glad when at last I saw walls to the left and to the right of me in the distance, but these long walls are closing in on each other so fast that I have already reached the last room, and there in the corner stands the trap I am heading for.'

22

What calls for interpretation in Kafka is his refusal to be interpreted, his evasiveness even in the realm of his own Negative.

97

The moment an attempt is made to read *into* the text, the reader brings from his own experience an otherworldly presence to the fiction that is the experiential equivalent of the fiction's "unfathomable fate."

It is only when the victim has at last understood what
the reader has known for some time and gives up his comi-
cally ineffectual gestures that Kafka joins his defeated victim, allowing the initial "K" to subsume them both in the
reader's awareness of a common condemnation. "Like a
dog!" is spoken for all mankind—for Joseph K., the author
and the reader.

17
And finally, after a night of the most anxious suspense, the
morning of the dreaded third arrived.

23
Might it have been blood? It seems that bloodstains can't be
completely removed, even with chemicals, and certainly not
with soap and water.

10
Why have I devoted so much attention to Kafka here?

61
The ventilation system was efficient, and cold air cut
through the men's socks and trousers like iced water. Cold
as a whore's tit. They responded by working harder, by
eager sawing and chopping. Let's get out of here as soon as
we can, was the watchword. They worked faster and faster, with dangerous lack of concern for their sharp knives.

20
Sometimes the corpse of an escaped prisoner was propped
up on a chair with a sign reading, "Here I am."

5
Not so loud you fool!

70

We had arranged to drive the Oder breach in order to watch
the last decisive offensive against Berlin. Long ago I had
picked out a hill on my property, an estate in a forest near
Eberswald, from which the territory along the Oder could be
viewed. Before the war I had intended to build a small country house there. Instead I had an observation trench dug on
the land.

55

Huzel remembers that he shouted at the official: Here I
stand, with the most important documents in Germany! And
I can't even find a place to put them. As he stormed toward
the door, the official called him back; he had just remem-
bered an old abandoned mine in the village of Dornten, ten
miles away.

30

One is reminded of Joseph K.'s desperate attempt to prove
that nothing has changed by pulling out his identity papers
and thrusting them before the eyes of his mysterious accu-
sers.

30

Subtlest and most evasive of all writers, Kafka remains the
severest and most harassing of the belated sages of what
will yet become the Jewish cultural tradition of the future.

20

Everything Kafka says can be taken down and used in evidence. He thinks it must always be evidence against him.

91

In his commentary on the Psalms, Origen quotes a 'Hebrew'
scholar, presumably a member of the Rabbinic Academy of
Caesarea, as saying that the Holy Scriptures are like a

large house with many, many rooms, and that outside each door lies a key—but it is not the right one. To find the right key that will open the doors—that is the great and arduous task. This story, dating from the height of the Talmudic era, may give an idea of Kafka's deep roots in the tradition of Jewish mysticism.

22
Day after tomorrow I leave for Berlin. In spite of insomnia, headaches and worries, perhaps in a better state than ever before.

7
This then is what happened next:

60
Two juveniles had broken into the apartment of an elderly couple, tied them up and robbed them. They gagged the seventy-year-old man, and he suffocated. Here the victims interested me more than the perpetrators. I had found out that the man had been a high ranking SS officer, and that some years earlier proceedings against him had been dropped.

15
Kafka's truth is not Kafka's world (no more Kafka-ism), but the signs of that world.

66
I had actually meant, he wrote to Milena, to go to Palestine in October. I think we talked about it, of course it would never have come off, it was a fantasy, the kind of fantasy someone has who is convinced that he will never again leave his bed. If I'm never going to leave my bed again, why shouldn't I travel as far as Palestine?

71

From the perspective of writing, as from that of a jealous divinity, everything appears to be stolen: even the body of words. The stealing makes the hand alive. The writer is an Argonaut; and style is but *argot*, thieves' slang, however sublime. Every *Aufhebung* perpetrated by this "light" hand, every elevation of sublimation, betrays the desire for a "s'avoir absolu" that would demonstrate—monstrously if need be—one's hand, style, presence.

46

I called this work *The Philosophy of 'As if'* because it seemed to me to express more convincingly than any other title what I wanted to say, namely that 'As if', i.e. appearance, the consciously false, plays an enormous part in science, in world-philosophies and in life.

47

What does "alive" mean in such conditions?
That was the problem. That was the whole problem.
But people were dying in the streets. There were bodies *everywhere.*
Exactly. That was the paradox.
You see it as a paradox?
I'm sure of it.
Why? Can you explain?
No.

41

This quasi-stoical attitude, this sudden activation of the mechanism whereby the Third Reich, real only yesterday, was derealized, also made it possible, in the second step, for Germans to identify themselves with the victors and without any sign of wounded pride.

66

But the hands of one of the partners were already at K.'s throat, while the other thrust the knife deep into his heart and turned it there twice. With failing eyes K. could still see the two of them immediately before him, cheek leaning against cheek, watching the final act. "Like a dog!" he said; it was as if the shame of it must outlive him.

March 7, 1989

99: THE NEW MEANING

59
It was an exquisite January morning in which there was no threat of rain, but a grey sky making the calmest background for the charms of a mild winter scene:—the grassy borders of the lanes, the hedgerows sprinkled with red berries and haunted with low twitterings, the purple bareness of the elms, the rich brown of the furrows.

15
The longing began in his speechless genitals, for which his brain cells acted as interpreter.

16
Who is it then?
No one, she said. I just don't know why I am alive.

13
Things aren't so jolly easy, said Philip, more to himself than to her.

10
I don't know. Yes I do. I'm scared to move.

51
This agreeable young woman, with her pleasant sexual
dreams, had been reborn within the breaking contours of her
crushed sports car. Three months later, sitting beside her
physiotherapist instructor in her new invalid car, she held
the chromium treadles in her strong fingers as if they were
extensions of her clitoris.

9
She stopped. Guess what the ending's going to be.

4
That's putting it disagreeably.

5
It was time to exit.

29
She thought: God, I've done it now. Broken my silence, the
last weapon I had. And replaced the glass, thinking: What
a fool I am to talk to him.

33
Juan liked to tell her stories with a certain artistic disorder,
while Tell seemed anxious to arrive at the conclusion immediately, probably in order to get back to the ecology of the
petrels.

48
Other voices, as if glad of the opening, murmured hasty
compassion. "Quite startling," "Monstrous," "Most painful
to see." The lank young man, with the eyeglass on a broad
ribbon, pronounced mincingly the word "Grotesque," whose

justness was appreciated by those standing near him. They smiled at each other.

62

Guest Four. He stands to make at least fifteen grand out of this, so what's the matter?
Guest Five. Who said anything was the matter?
Guest One. No, it's really true, really. She took him home to her flat. He was so excited he could hardly get up the stairs.
Guest Six. I have three showers a day — absolutely every day.

27

The bridge of steps: how to make love there in
twenty-five different positions
so as to have a happy and rosy complexion later at
the "Captain's Table."

16

Poetry, despite its publicists, is not a struggle against repression but itself a kind of repression.

7

He probes the details, over and over.

49

get no answer: which journeys what is she doing where does she live and what of her enemies did she love her deep-voiced doctor and whether it is important how old was she when her virginity and for whom apart from orange her favorite color can she cook

25
Wasn't his body after all, exploiting the capital formation of his thoughts, thriving on surplus value of his mind, and gorging itself on his will?

20
Good Gods! That set me off again. I certainly expect that, and I hope it won't be long in coming.

58
I know now that I am no longer waiting, and that the previous part of my life in which I thought I was waiting and therefore only half-alive was not waiting, although it was tinged with expectancy, but living under and into this reply which has suddenly caused everything in my world to take on a new meaning.

53
I had consistently mastered her predicament: she had at once to cultivate contacts, so that people shouldn't guess her real concentration, and to make them a literal touch and go, so that they shouldn't suspect the enfeeblement of her mind. It was obviously still worth everything to her that she was so charming.

63
I didn't teach your class the next day. As every fifteen days, on Wednesday from three to four, instead of being with you, I was with my seventh-graders, on the main floor, making them recite the lessons of the day before about the religion, the temples and the tombs of ancient Egypt, before transporting them to the other tip of the fertile crescent.

18
In short I floated through a sea of regulations, codes and religious machinations like a fish through water.

28
July 11? 12? 1862—sinking deeper and deeper into sexual deliriums—obsessed by fantasies of hanging and death in orgasms—Once in India I saw a man hanged.

6
Sarah laughed. You're making it up.

31
Marianne. Evidently. . . it's funny in French. . . in the end, words often mean the opposite to what they are supposed to mean. We say 'evident' about things that aren't evident at all.

6
(knocking a pipe, was he offensive)

19
They glanced back at me, speaking in low tones. Nothing, I thought, can break the whiteness of our voices.

25
For fully five minutes I must have sat inert, exhausted, as though I myself had been a third combatant in the deathly struggle recently concluded.

20
No—there isn't enough time to do it right. There was never enough time to do it right, I said.

14
They are too preoccupied, too indifferent to anything that does not regard them personally.

3
Look she said.

74
A shower of rockets rose in the sky, and soon, reaching the
height of their ascent, their glowing cases burst with a
sharp bang, scattering through space a thousand luminous
portraits of the young Baron Ballisterous, which it was
intended should be substituted for the normal, commonplace
succession of rain and stars. Each image as it burst from
its case, unfolded of its own accord, to float at large, with a
gentle swaying motion.

62
Can one—at least, could one ever—begin to write without
taking oneself for another? For the history of sources we
should substitute the history of figures: the origin of the
work is not the first influence, it is the first posture: one
copies a role, then by metonymy, or art: I begin by repro-
ducing the person I want to be.

53
Marco was just impractical, an absolutely helpless man. All
that he could do was to copy ancient things and write about
them. His mind was completely in it. All practical affairs
of life seemed impossible to him, such a simple matter of
finding food or buying a railway ticket seemed a monumen-
tal job.

69
He was a tall, fair-haired pink faced young man, slightly
bald. He could not have been more than thirty. He spoke in
a slow, serious voice, which often rose to a shrill, feminine
pitch and died away in that delicate whisper, or, as Gerard
de Nerval says of Sylvia, that FRISSON MODULE, in
which lies so much of the charm of the Oxford accent, now,
alas, no longer fashionable.

19

He asked for descriptions of where I worked, the city and its surroundings and the people I had met.

52

Brown envelopes of blue pictures? he repeated. He never said a dickey bird to me, now, about any blue pictures. He grinned, and then an uncertain memory floated back. Wait now, I tell a lie. Back in summer, he told me he had a good tickle going for him, do you see.

13

This takes up a Saturday morning in the department stores around Herald Square.

17

Maybe he was getting warmer, but his look or wish was turned before it got far enough.

7

How was the small dining room lit?

37

Thus we sat and I kept up my persuasive drone; I am a bad speaker, and the oration which I seem to render word for word did not flow with the lissom glide it has on paper.

24

Nature!
Why do you start?
I know not, with a sort of shudder, but I have heard of a book entitled NATURE IN DISEASE.

24

Startled, Paul looked at her and said in a frightened voice:
How do you know that?

I don't know it.
You've just said it.

16
Let it go at that, for the moment. I will write about her
motives later, perhaps.

56
The autumn sky was pure and lofty, it was the sky of
France. It was the sky of the paradise lost which hadn't
come true in Beaulieu-sur-Loire. What color was the sky
above the true paradise, the one the little Christian had

been given on the crooked side of the saber? Or didn't that
paradise exist?

73
I'm aware that a good many perfectly intelligent people
can't stand parenthetical comments while a story's purport-
edly being told. (We're advised of these things by mail—
mostly, granted, by thesis preparers with very good na-
tured, oaty urges to write us under the table in their off-
campus time. But we read, and usually we believe; good,
bad, or indifferent, any string of English words holds our
attention as if they came from Prospero himself.)

75
Knowing he was coming, Peggy had decided against sunglasses, a sign of trust to leave them off. Her walleyes are
naked to him, her face has this helpless look, turned full
toward him while both eyes seem fascinated by something in
the corners of the ceiling. He knows one eye is bad but can
never bring himself to figure out which. And all around her
eyes this net of white wrinkles the sunglasses usually con-
ceal.

25
My dear birdie, who ever expected to see you! I thought you
fluttered in only now and then, to see how everything was
getting on—

63
I hesitate to admit it for fear of using a few more naughty
words: it seems to me that at that time I felt the need for
love. Obscene, isn't it? In any case I experienced a secret
suffering, a sort of privation that made me emptier and
allowed me, partly through obligation and partly out of curiosity, to make a few commitments.

51
On the white plate, a land crab spreads out its five pairs of
clearly jointed, muscular legs. Around its mouth, many similar appendages are arranged in pairs. The creature used
them to produce a kind of crackling sound, audible at close
range, like that which the Scutigera makes in certain cases.

29
What are you doing? she panted. Are you mad? At last the
top of her dress dropped to her waist, leaving her breasts
exposed, large and white, bluishly white.

18
After he had left the room, she thought: I am more than
twice as old as he is.

11
So where does that leave you?
Out.
Where will you go?

9
Once more I was forced to admit my ignorance.

56

Bill switched off the lights, reversed the car in the road, and headed back eastward. It took ten minutes to reach the turning. There a faded half board on a drunken post read KAYLABIIOMIN, and underneath PRIVA. The right part of the board had disappeared. A dirt road led North. VK said, this is it.

78

Later, much later, speaking in whispers in order not to wake Bill, I tell her about our former stay in the desert. Not my first time, but the second time with Bill and Inge. . . I feel so tired, so very tired, she says almost apologetically as she lies down beside me. The next morning Bill asks if we had made love. When I refuse to tell him, he angrily leaves the room, slamming the door shut behind him.

42

Human beings are tiny centers of consciousness in the void, with only their frail bodies to keep out the overpowering nothing of infinity which presses in on them—little creatures growing and building against the annihilation of space and the inorganic world.

37

So, so. A WANDERVOGEL in the mountains of Pain. He's been going on for much too long, he has chosen the game for nothing if not for the kind of end it will bring him. NICHT WAHR?

9

Quite moving, especially for a mind seemingly so uncultivated.

18
I was about to ask him what he meant by this, when he took me by the sleeve.

47
Author's Additional Note
The sole vestige of the guitarist-singer-composer Jean-Pierre Suc, who committed suicide on the Paris-Montpellier train in 1960, and with whom I used to pass an evening from time to time at a nightclub in the quarter, is a deluxe condom terminating in a hand.

44
Like all kinds of partitionings, it makes me feel that there is something wrong. And this same uneasiness suddenly brings me back to a restaurant (Le Véfour, to be exact), at the moment when a perfectly anonymous head-waiter pours fruity wine into my glass.

13
I filled my cigarette case; lightweight, thin and elegant, covered with black leather.

4
For God's sake, doubt.

36
With only a few feet between us, virtually within reach of one another, I made my presence apparent by rattling the magazine pages, coughing, swearing, casting ambiguous phrases at the ceiling, and repeatedly looking at him.

43
Everything that can be said has been said many times. I have no new observations to make. The decisions he faces have been tormenting him for decades.

If after all I—
But he cannot finish the sentence. We both know what is
meant.

64
—We both know. It's been going on for a month. Things
get around fast among us. We know. . . Large low clouds
came drifting in from the open sea, but the point still lay in
the sun. The shadow of a tamarisk drew an uneven fringe
on the sand which was not replacing the chalky lumps and
angular pebbles in the stretch of road behind.

12
Why the hell can't you leave my man alone? he almost
shouted.

41
He reached for a paper knife on the piano and placed the
point of it on my diaphragm. He traced an imaginary line of
incision and flourished the knife before my eyes. That's how
I'll begin, he said, in your guts.

37
Deliberately I avoided making any plans. I would leave
everything to the inspiration of the moment. I had vaguely
expected that my excitement and desperation would, when
the time came, provide me with some daring, amazing idea.

57
I went with the pull. In passing I blocked his left foot from
behind, grabbed his shirt and heard it tear. Something hit
me on the neck, but it wasn't metal. I spun to the left and
he went over sideways and landed catlike on his feet again
before I had any kind of balance.

29
Let me explain. Imagine that something happened—say an assault—and someone comes in immediately afterwards. What happened? asks the visitor. Help. Moans, cries, and so forth. What happened?

56
But indeed these qualities account for our charm, our good humor, our handsome physiques, our arrogance, our explosive servility. We are what we wish to be. We would have it no other way. Our national type is desirable as well as inescapable. You and I? You and I are two perfect examples of our national type.

25
Huh? Am I bleeding again?
Tak took him by the chin and turned his face.
You sure are, and pressed another towel to his head.

19
How should I retrace my route on a map—how above all, identify this place we are now entering. . . ?

23
Far below one catches an occasional glimpse of the nearly black carpet of forest, rent by ribbon-like slashes that gleam brightly as bronze.

43
I'd been reading the steam. And at the same time I was having a fantastic "Holy City Seizure." And with no cloud machine and no Diana Vienna!
    White globs!
    I yelled into the mouthpiece. "Who are you?"
    More globs. . . smear chest and buttocks. . .

43

A child will be able to construct and understand utterances which are, at the same time, acceptable sentences in his language. At every moment of our lives we formulate and understand a host of sentences different from any that we have heard before.

3

Twenty years later.

18

The man was burying my feet in the sand. It was on the beach at Mellila. I remember.

10

Where had he come from. How had he got there?

9

I hadn't thought I might never come back here?

17

One or more romantic melodramas in which improbability will become an active and concrete element of poetry.

8

Suppose the deception goes even further than that?

27

I managed to climb the steps of the pedestal on which the statue in the middle of the square was perched. From that vantage point I shouted.

7

I don't know—I don't know anything.

47
I proposed various solutions, all of them inadequate. We discussed them. Finally Stephen Albert said: In a guessing game to which the answer is chess, which word is the only one prohibited?
I thought for a moment and then replied: The word is chess. Precisely, said Albert.

11
I decided to follow the letter in case it got lost.

31
Behind him the Station-master writes something in a large elongated ledger, and as he does so, glances up at the clock over the Track 2 Gate 9:29. Nice evening, he says.

18
Take the path directly opposite to that which is in use and you will almost always do right.

73
I was never quite taken in by this "automatic writing." But I have enjoyed the game for its own sake: an only son, I would play it alone. Now and then, I used to stop writing and pretend to hesitate so that I could feel I was, with my

furrowed brow and far-away look, A WRITER. Besides, I adored plagiarism, through snobbery, and I deliberately carried it to extremes, as will be seen.

43
Today I am to see the Dalai Lama. . . but meanwhile the world goes on, and finance booms (zooms). We have run out of toilet paper and are using Saturday's newspaper. I become absorbed in the news of business—too good to pass over.

4
Good God! You're mad!

35
The enclosure was plunged in complete silence, a silence at once heavy and full of suspense, which the faint wild-beast smell that hung in the air seemed to endow with a significance of anguished expectancy.

39
A light rain started to fall, and dawn was breaking as they turned off the main road, wound their way through the narrow streets of a village out into the open country, and began driving slowly through a forest.

8
Well, of course it's over. Here I am!

7
That's my name. I've always been Foster.

This book was designed by Keith and Rosmarie Waldrop and set in 12 pt. Century Schoolbook. It was printed on 60 lb. Glatfelter (an acid-free paper) and smyth-sewn by Thomson-Shore in Dexter, MI. There are 3000 copies, of which 450 are clothbound, and 50 clothbound and signed.